The Ugly Duckling

A DORLING KINDERSLEY BOOK

First American Edition, 1994
2 4 6 8 10 9 7 5 3

Published in the United States by
Dorling Kindersley Publishing, Inc., 95 Madison Avenue
New York, New York 10016

Library of Congress Cataloging-in-Publication Data
Mitchell, Adrian. 1932-
The Ugly Duckling / retold by Adrian Mitchell ; illustrated by
Jonathan Heale.—1st American ed.
p.   cm.
Summary: An ugly duckling spends an unhappy year ostracized
by the other animals before he grows into a beautiful swan.
ISBN. 1-56458-557-3
[1. Fairy tales.] I. Heale, Jonathan, ill.
II. Andersen, H.C. (Hans Christian), 1805-1875. Grimme ælling III. Title
PZ8.M67Ug   1994
[E]—dc20
93-39962
CIP
AC

Color reproduction by DOT Gradations Ltd.
Printed in Hong Kong by
South China Printing Company (1988) Limited

The Ugly Duckling

by

HANS CHRISTIAN ANDERSEN

retold by Adrian Mitchell

&

with woodcuts by Jonathan Heale

Deep in the countryside
Everything was beautiful.
Summertime—
The oats were green, the wheat was golden,
And the new haystacks in the meadow
Smelled of sugar and bonfire smoke.
The old Stork tottered around on his long red legs,
Talking to himself in Egyptian
(Which he was taught by his dear old mother).

All around the meadow
Stood a forest of shadows.
Hidden in the middle of the trees
Lay a secret lake.
Yes, deep in the countryside
Everything was beautiful.

An ancient castle sat in the sunshine
Surrounded by a pea-green moat.
By its crumbly walls grew giant hogweeds,
So high that children could walk under their leaves.
In this wild place a Duck had built her nest.
And she sat there, under a giant hogweed,
With very few visitors, hatching her eggs.

At last her eggs began to crack open.
First one "Cheep! Cheep!" then another "Cheep!"
And suddenly all the eggs were alive
And little heads were popping out. "Cheep! Cheep!"
"Quack! Quack!" said their mother,
And out they all scrambled,
Blinking up at the giant hogweed.
Their mother Duck let them stare and stare,
For green is very good for the eyes.

All the Ducklings cheeped, "What a great big world!"
(They had so much more room now than inside those eggs.)
"Oh, the world's much wider than this," said their mother.
"It goes beyond the moat, right over the meadow.
But nobody's ever been that far.
Now, have you all been born?"
She looked around. "All except one,
And that's the biggest egg of them all—
Oh no!" And she fluffed her feathers out
And sat down grumpily on the great egg.

"How did the hatching go?"
Asked an elderly Duck-aunt, paying a visit.
"Well, this one egg just won't crack.
But the rest are handsome Ducklings, just like their father,
That no-good fly-by-night—
You know, he never comes to see me."

"That big one's probably a turkey's egg,"
Said the elderly Duck-aunt.
"I was once bamboozled like that.
Turkeys are hopeless. Scared of water.
Yes, that's a turkey's egg all right.
Let it lie there—teach the others to swim."
"No, I think I'll keep trying," said the Duck.
"None of my business," said the elderly Duck-aunt
As she swam away with her bill in the air.

At last the great egg cracked and broke open.
"Cheep? Cheep?" The new Duckling tumbled out.
He was very big. He was very ugly.
The mother Duck looked him over from bow to stern.
"He's enormous," she thought.
"Better go swimming tomorrow.
Then we'll find out if he's a turkey."

The next day the sun shone on the giant hogweed.
Mother Duck and all her children
Waddled down to the pea-green moat.
Splash! She was swimming. "Quack!" she called,
And one by one the Ducklings jumped in.
Their heads dipped under, but then they bobbed back up
And they began to paddle around busily,
All together—even the ugly one.

"He can't be a turkey," thought his mother.
"He moves his legs well. What a straight neck!
He's my own child and not too bad-looking."
Then she said, "Come on out, little ones!
Follow me out into the wide world.
I'm going to show you the Great Duckyard.
Now, stay close behind me at all times
Or somebody may tread on your head!
And, whatever you do, watch out for the Cat!"

So they waddled into the Duckyard
Where two families were quarreling
Over who should have a dusty eel's head—
But in the end the Cat ran away with it.

"That's life," said the mother Duck,
But her mouth watered. She'd have liked that eel.
"Come along, children, walk properly.
Bow politely to the Duchess Duck,
For she is the most important Duck
In the entire Duckyard."

"Why's she so fat?" asked the Ugly Duckling.
"Shh!" said his mother. "She has Spanish blood.
She's respected by everyone, men and animals.
Keep your toes turned out and your legs apart!"
They all bowed to the Duchess and said, "Quack!"

But a crowd of Ducks kept staring and said,
"Have we really got to put up with this?
The Duckyard's already overcrowded.
That odd Duckling's far too ugly for us!"
Then a skinny young Drake flew straight at the Duckling
And pecked him hard on the neck.

"Leave him alone!" shouted the mother Duck.
"He's not hurting you."
"He couldn't hurt me, he's too big and weird,"
Answered the skinny young Drake.
"What he needs is a good old bashing."

"A nice-looking brood," murmured the Duchess Duck,
"All except that one. He's a mistake.
Why not pop him back into his egg,
Glue it together, and hatch him again?"

"It can't be done, Your Grace," said his mother.
"But perhaps he'll grow up to be smaller."
She pecked him lightly and smoothed his feathers.
"Looks don't count so much with a Drake.
He's a strong little lad. I think he'll get by."

"Well," said the Duchess, "the rest are pretty enough.
You can make yourselves at home in my Duckyard
And if you ever find anything like an eel's head—
Don't forget the Duchess!"

After that they all settled down.
But the Ugly Duckling was bitten and teased
By all the Ducks—the Hens as well.
"Too big! Too big!" they squawked at him.
The poor Duckling didn't know where to turn.

The bullying went on all the first day.
Every day it got worse and worse.
They all chased him. His brothers and sisters shouted
"Fishface! Fishface! The Cat's going to eat you!"
Even his own mother said to him,
"I sometimes wish you lived somewhere else."
All the Ducks bit him, all the Hens scratched him,
And the girl who fed the poultry each morning
Always gave him a kick for breakfast.

One day he flew over the Duckyard fence
And the Sparrows perching on top of it
Fluttered up, twittering in terror.
"It's because I'm so ugly," thought the Duckling,
And he shut his eyes and flew on and on
Till he came to the marsh where the Wild Ducks live.
There he lay all night long, tired, sorry, and sad.

At dawn the Wild Ducks flocked around him.
"What kind of bird are you supposed to be?"
The Duckling turned himself round and round,
Bowing politely in all directions.
"You're ugly," they said, "but that doesn't matter.
So long as you don't want to marry our daughters."
The poor Duckling didn't want to get married,
He just wanted to lie down and sleep in the reeds.

For two days and nights he lay in the marshes.
On the third day, two Wild Ganders landed.
"Listen, boy," they said, "You're so ugly that we like you.
Fly along with us. You'll enjoy migration.
There's a swamp over there full of Wild Geese,
The sweetest little creatures who ever hissed.
You're so ugly that you might strike lucky."

Bang! Bang! The Wild Ganders fell dead,
Marsh water reddening around their bodies.
Bang! Bang! again. Out of the swamp
Flew a flock of Wild Geese.
Bang! It was a big hunting party:
Hunters in bushes. Hunters up trees.
Blue gunsmoke floated like ghosts through the branches,
Drifting away across the waters.

Retrievers came splashing through the mud,
Squashing the bulrushes.
The Duckling hid his head under his wing.
Then the steaming muzzle of a terrible Dog
Pushed itself into the Duckling's face.
Its tongue hung dripping from its mouth.
Its brown eyes glittered wickedly.
It opened a cave of sharp yellow teeth and—
Splish-splash! It bounded off
Without touching one of the Duckling's feathers.

"I'm so ugly, even a dog won't eat me,"
Thought the Duckling. He lay very still.
And Bang! The shooting went on and on.
It was late in the day when the hunters went home.
But even then, the Duckling lay still.
Finally he stood up, shook his feathers,
And scurried away from the marshes.
A storm arose, but he staggered on,
Over fields, down ditches, through hedges and thickets.

Night fell as he reached a ramshackle shack.
It was so crooked it couldn't decide
Which way it should collapse. So it stayed standing,
A puzzled little hut.
The wind now blew so ferociously
That the Duckling had to sit on his own tail
To stop himself from being blown away.
Then he noticed the shack's door had only one hinge,
So it hung askew, leaving a duck-sized gap.

The Ugly Duckling squeezed himself through
Into that ramshackle shack.
An old woman lived in that hut
With her Tomcat, Sonny,
Who could arch his back and purr
And give off electric sparks
(But only if you stroked him the wrong way).
She had a Hen called Shtumpig
Because she had such short legs.
She laid excellent eggs and the old woman
Loved Shtumpig like a baby.

In the morning they noticed the strange Duckling.
Sonny purred and Shtumpig clucked.
"What's up?" asked the old woman.
She was shortsighted and mistook the Duckling
For a grown-up Duck who'd lost her way.
"What good luck! We'll all have duck eggs,
So long as it isn't a Drake. We'll see.
You can stay with us, on trial, for three weeks."

But three weeks passed and no eggs appeared.
Now Sonny the Tomcat thought he was king,
And Shtumpig the Hen acted like a queen.
The Duckling wasn't sure that this was fair.
But Shtumpig asked him, "Can you lay eggs?"
"No."
"Then you'd better keep your bill shut."
And Sonny asked, "Can you arch your back?
Can you purr? Can you give off electric sparks?"
"No."
"Then your opinions aren't worth a feather."

So the Duckling squashed himself into a corner
Feeling sad and sorry for himself.
Then he thought of the sky and the bright sun
And he longed to go swimming
With a longing so great he nearly exploded.
"What's wrong with you?" asked Shtumpig. "Swimming?
You sit around doing nothing all day,
That's why you come up with these outlandish notions!
Lay an egg or do some purring—
You'll soon feel normal again."

"But it's wonderful, floating on a lake.
It's great when the water closes over your head
And you dive right down to the muddy bottom!"

"Yes, I'm sure it's heavenly!" said Shtumpig.
"You're crazy. Ask Sonny—he's a very wise cat—
Ask him if he feels like swimming.
Ask the old woman—she's even wiser—
If she wants to go diving, nose-down in the mud!"
"You don't understand me," the Duckling said.

"You think you're more clever than the Cat
And the old woman and me?" asked Shtumpig the Hen.
"Be grateful we allow you to enjoy
Our highly intelligent company.
You're an ignoramus and a bore!
I only tell you for your own good,
Because true friends always speak the honest truth.
Now why won't you even bother to purr
Or lay the odd egg?"

"I think I'll go out into the wide world,"
Said the Ugly Duckling.

"Well, go on then," said Shtumpig the Hen.

So off went the Duckling.
He hurried through the forest of shadows
To the shore of the secret lake.
He swam and dived in the cool water,
But the other waterbirds turned away
Because he was so ugly.

Autumn arrived. The forest leaves
Turned yellow and brown and danced down from the trees.
The sky was dark purple, ready to snow.
A Raven sat on the forest fence
And croaked with cold till his throat was sore.
And the Duckling shivered, all by himself.

One evening at sunset,
When the sky was bright as orange juice,
A flock of great, handsome birds flew up out of the reeds.
The Duckling had never seen such beauty.
Dazzling white, with long, bending necks,
They were Swans.

They gave a mysterious cry, spread their wings wide
And flew far away from that cold country,
Over the ocean, toward warmer lands.
Higher and higher they flew. The Duckling's heart
Was full to bursting with new feelings.
He splashed around and around like a waterwheel.
He stretched his neck after the Swans and gave
Such an odd, loud hoot that he made himself jump.
He would never forget those beautiful birds.

They were gone. He plunged down to the mud of the lake.
When he finally surfaced, he was all alone.
He didn't know that the Swans were called Swans.
He didn't know where they were flying to,
But he was full of love for them.
It wasn't that he envied them—
How could he think of being so beautiful?
He'd have been contented back in the Duckyard
If only the others had stopped picking on him.

The winter grew colder. Ice covered the lake.
The Duckling had to keep swimming in circles
To keep the water from freezing completely.
Every night his swimming hole became smaller.
He smashed at the ice with his red webbed feet,
But it crackled and gripped him till he lay exhausted,
Body all stiff, frozen fast in the ice.

Early the next morning a farmer came by.
He smashed the ice with a wooden clog
And carried the Duckling back to his warm kitchen,
Where the Duckling gradually came back to life.

The children wanted to play with him,
But the Duckling, terrified, jumped in the milk bucket,
Flapping milk all over the room.
The farmer's wife yelled and clapped her hands,
So the Duckling flew into a tub of soft butter,
Then in and out of a barrel of flour.
He looked like a clown dressed up as a ghost.
The farmer's wife threw the poker at him.
The children tumbled over each other,
Laughing, trying to catch the Duckling.
Luckily somebody left the door open,
So he scooted out and hid himself
Deep in the snow-covered undergrowth.

To list all the pains the Duckling endured
In that long winter would only make you miserable.
He lay in the bulrushes by the secret lake
Till the sun started shining and the larks began to sing.
And suddenly it was springtime.

All at once the Duckling spread out his wings.
They beat the air more powerfully now,
And up he flew, across the secret lake,
And down into a sloping garden
With apple trees in blossom
And sweet-smelling lilac trees
Dangling their long branches in the lake.
Such lovely, early April brightness!

Out of the rushes swam three beautiful Swans.
They rustled their wings, moving lightly on the water.
The Duckling recognized them with a sad heart.
"I'll fly over to those fine birds,"
Said the Duckling to himself.
"They may peck me to death for being so ugly
And for daring to approach them,
But I'd rather be killed by such marvelous birds
Than bitten by Ducks and scratched by Hens
And kicked every morning by the poultry girl."

So he flew onto the water
And he swam toward the wonderful Swans.
And they saw him and came gliding toward him
With their fine wings outstretched.
"Kill me," said the Duckling, bowing his head.
But what did he see down in the clear lake?

His own reflection. And look at it!
He wasn't an ugly, horrible, clumsy beast.
He was . . . a Swan!

What does it matter if you're born in a Duckyard
So long as you're hatched from the egg of a Swan?

Some children ran down the sloping garden
To throw bits of bread into the lake.
The smallest shouted, "There's a new one!"
All the children said, "Yes, a new Swan!"
And they clapped and jumped around
And ran off to fetch their mother and father.
They all came back with pieces of cake
And scattered the crumbs on the water.
(The smallest one said that it was now Lake Cake.)
And everyone said, "The new Swan's the best.
He's so handsome! So bright and beautiful!"
And all the older Swans bowed down to him.

He felt shy and hid his head under his wing
For he didn't know where to put himself.
He felt completely happy, but not at all proud.
He remembered how once he was bullied and despised,
But now everyone called him beautiful.

The lilac trees stretched out their branches to him.
The sun shone warmly on the feathers of his back.
He shook his strong wings
And raised his graceful neck
And cried out from the bottom of his heart,
"I never dreamed of so much happiness
When I was the Ugly Duckling!"